The Good,
the Bad and
the Very Slimy

Look for these

ROTTEN SCHOOL
books, too!

The Big
Blueberry
Barf-Off!

The Great
Smelling Bee

ROTTEN SCHOOL

The Good, the Bad and the Very Slimy

R.L. STINE

Illustrations by Trip Park

HarperCollinsPublishers

A Parachute Press Book

For Hampton
–TP

Library of Congress Cataloging-in-Publication Data
Stine, R. L.
The good, the bad and the very slimy / R.L. Stine ; illustrations by Trip Park.
p. cm. — (Rotten School ; 3)
"A Parachute Press Book."
Summary: Rotten School's bad boy, Bernie B., is trying to turn over a new leaf in
order to date the prettiest girl in school, but he may trip over his own slime trail.
ISBN-10: 0-06-078592-6 (trade bdg.) — ISBN-10: 0-06-078593-4 (lib. bdg.)
ISBN-13: 978-0-06-078592-5 (trade bdg.) — ISBN-13: 978-0-06-078593-2 (lib. bdg.)
1. Boarding schools—Fiction. 2. Schools—Fiction. 3. Slugs (Mollusks)—Fiction.]
I. Park, Trip, ill. II. Title. III. Series.
PZ7.S86037Go 2005   2005007696
[Fic]—dc22   CIP
                                                                            AC

Cover and interior design by mjcdesign
1 2 3 4 5 6 7 8 9 10

First Edition

CONTENTS

Morning Announcements 1

1. A Brand-New Bernie 4

2. Our Mystery Science Experiment ... 11

3. "She's Not My Girlfriend!" 14

4. The Magic Moment 19

5. April-May Says Yes 24

6. Belzer Has a Problem 27

7. My Good Deed 30

8. Crushed 33

9. Sherman Shows Off 36

10. Crushed, Part Two 42

11. Jennifer Attacks 45

12. My First Night as a Bookworm 50

13. How I Impressed April-May 55

14. I'm Tense 60

15. I'm Hot! 63

16. The Double-Smart Quiz Bowl 69

17. Billy the Brain 75

18. A Champion Slug 79

19. The Good, the Bad
     and the Very Slimy 83

20. Bernie Thinks Fast 88

21. The Old Garden Hose Trick 93

22. Victory! 97

23. Mrs. Heinie Steps In 104

24. Could It Get Any Worse? 108

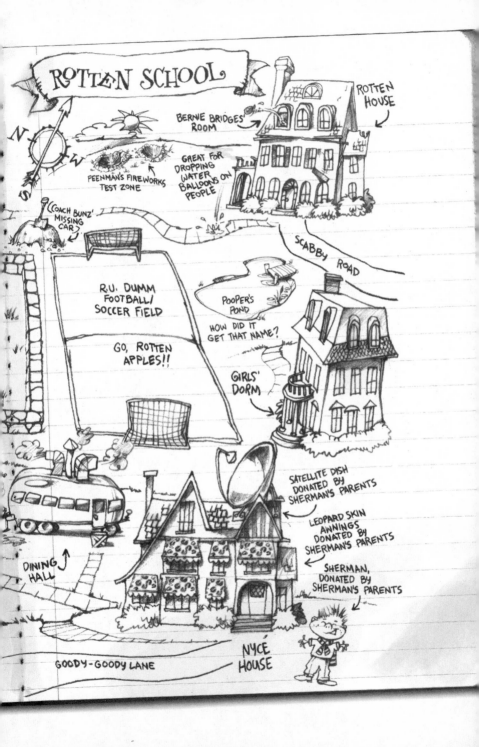

MORNING ANNOUNCEMENTS

Good morning, Rotten Students. This is Head-master Upchuck with your Morning Announcements, which I read over the loudspeaker every morning at this time.

If you are absent today, I'm sorry you are missing these announcements. And I don't really know why I'm talking to you since you're not here.

For those of you who are here, I hope you will stop your insane jabbering and listen carefully. And Have a Rotten Day....

Congratulations to Mr. Boring's fifth-grade Science class for proving beyond a doubt that cats cannot float.

The Sixth-Grade Photography Club would like to apologize to Mrs. Lintpocket, dorm mother of Nyce House, for the candid photos they took through her window, titled, *Woman in the Shower*.

Congratulations to Coach Bunz and our Rotten Apples softball team for three straight games without an injury.

The Saturday afternoon cake sale has been canceled because some thoughtless person played a joke and switched the cake flour with cement.... Please be careful, students. We are sorry to announce that the new skating rink is unsafe— because it was built with cake flour.

Important Warning: Those bottles stolen from Nurse Hanley's office yesterday are not apple juice. They are urine samples.

Nurse Hanley would also like to remind all students that the No Drinking from the Tropical Fish Aquarium rule will be strictly enforced.

Mrs. Heinie would like to remind fourth graders that it is book report time. Please remember that books in the *Rotten School* book series cannot be used for book reports. Those books should not be brought to school.

Chef Baloney is working his magic in the kitchen again. The menu for tonight's dinner in the dining hall will feature Squid Loaf in a hearty Saliva Sauce.

Chapter 1

A BRAND-NEW BERNIE

You are probably wondering why I—Bernie Bridges—decided to change my behavior, change my personality, and become a whole new kid.

A *new* Bernie Bridges! It's a frightening thought—isn't it?

Especially since the *old* Bernie Bridges was *perfect*!

Well, the new Bernie Bridges had to be even perfecter. You'll see why....

Don't get me wrong. I think life is great here at the Rotten School. I think all kids should go to

4

boarding school and live away from home.

My buddies and I live in an old house at the back of the campus, called Rotten House. No parents! It's a terrific life.

Of course, we *do* have some problems with those goody-goody kids who live in the dorm across from us. It's called Nyce House. What kind of geek would live in a place called *Nyce* House?

But, I'm getting away from my story. And I know you're very eager to hear my story—since it's all about *me*....

It started one night after dinner in the Student Center. That's where my guys and I go every night to shoot some pool, play video games, and hang out.

I was hurrying to the game room. Tuesday night is slug race night, and I was late. I had Sluggo, my racing slug, wrapped up safely in my shirt pocket.

I carried Sluggo into the game room and started to unwrap his little velvet blanket. The guys were waiting around the pool table.

I saw my pals Feenman and Crench standing behind me. They were holding up signs to cheer us on.

"Hey, Bernie, you're late," Feenman cried.

"No problem," I said, rolling my big slug around in my hand. "Sluggo is feeling strong tonight. And fast. *Aren't* you, Sluggo?"

He oozed a warm liquid into my hand. I guess he was trying to answer me.

That spoiled brat, Sherman Oaks—my arch-enemy—grinned across the table at me. He was petting a fat, silvery slug.

He had his buddies from the Nyce House dorm with him.

The big, beefy hulk, Joe Sweety, leaned over the table, putting his slug through its warm-up exercises. Wes Updood stood next to him, tossing his slug up in the air and catching it.

My friend Beast flashed me a thumbs-up. Beast is very big and very hairy. He grunts a lot, and sometimes he walks on all fours. But we're pretty sure he's human. (At least *80 percent* human.)

Nosebleed, another kid from my dorm, leaned against the wall with his head tilted back, trying to stop a nosebleed.

I set Sluggo down on the table and started to

give him a rubdown. We all train our own slugs. We race them from one end of the pool table to the other. Sometimes the slugs forget they are in a race. So we poke them with toothpicks to keep them moving. (They don't seem to mind.)

I turned to Sherman. "Sluggo has won five races in a row," I said. "He's going to leave your new slug in his slime trail."

Sherman shook his perfect, wavy blond hair. "I don't think so, Bernie. I brought a secret weapon tonight."

He plopped a white paper bag on the table—and pulled out a big hunk of raw meat. "Hamburger," he said. "It's gone rotten. See? It's turning green and purple. My slug, Godzilla, loves it. I put the spoiled meat at the end of the table. And Godzilla races his heart out to get to it."

"Yuck! It STINKS!" Feenman and Crench both cried. They covered their noses. "It's covered with MAGGOTS! Get it *out* of here!"

"This is top-grade sirloin," Sherman bragged. "Nothing but the best rotten meat for Godzilla."

I shook my head. "Sluggo still wins," I said. "He's

a vegetarian. He doesn't care about rotten meat."

I lined Sluggo up at the edge of the table. The big guy was eager to race. "Put up your money, dudes," I said. We each bet five dollars. It's winner-take-all— and we *know* who the winner will be!

Sherman plopped the pukey hunk of beef at the far end of the pool table. Then he placed his fat slug next to mine. Now all six slugs were lined up.

"Ready...," I called out. "Set..."

The game room door burst open.

We all spun around.

There stood Mrs. Heinie, our teacher, hands on her hips, her eyes bulging in horror behind those two-inch-thick glasses she wears.

"What on *earth* are you boys doing?" she shrieked.

Chapter 2

OUR MYSTERY SCIENCE EXPERIMENT

I tucked Sluggo into my shirt pocket. The other guys grabbed their slugs and shoved them out of sight.

"You look wonderful tonight, Mrs. H.," I said. I flashed her my big smile with the adorable dimples. "Is that a new scarf?"

"Cut the flattery, Bernie," she said. "I'm not wearing a scarf. My neck is wrinkled."

"It suits you!" I cried. "We didn't know it was you, Mrs. H. We thought it was a movie star."

Mrs. Heinie is our fourth-grade teacher. And she's our dorm mother at Rotten House. That means her job is to snoop and spy on us and keep us from having fun.

She sniffed the air and groaned. "What's that awful smell? Are you going to tell me what you boys are doing in here?"

Think fast, Bernie. Think fast.

I grabbed the pile of rotting meat and held it up to her. "It's for Science class," I said.

The other guys all nodded. "Yeah. Science class."

She squinted at us behind the thick glasses. "Go on. Explain."

"Well…," I started. "Mr. Boring, our science teacher, does a unit called Mysteries of Science. And we're…uh…doing our Mysteries of Science homework."

"Homework?" she said, studying us one by one. "That's a disgusting piece of rotting hamburger. How is that your homework?"

"We don't know," I said. "It's a *mystery*."

"Yeah. It's a Mystery of Science," Feenman said. He pulled off a chunk of meat and pretended to study it.

"We don't really know what we're studying," I

said. "Mr. Boring doesn't know, either. It's all a Mystery of Science."

I passed out hunks of the disgusting raw meat to the other guys. "Check it out, dudes. Make sure you get a piece with maggots crawling on it. Mr. Boring said that's very important."

Mrs. Heinie rolled her eyes. "Nice try," she said. I don't think she believed us.

She waved a finger at me. "Bernie, I'm watching you," she said. "That's a warning. I'm keeping my eye on you."

She turned and hurried away, holding her nose.

I waited till she was out of sight. Then I dropped the putrid hamburger on the floor. "Let's get outta here," I said. "I—I can't breathe. It *stinks* so bad!"

Sherman held up his slug. "What about the race?"

"Next Tuesday," I said. "Give the smell a chance to go away."

Holding my breath, I started to leave. Everyone came running out—except for Beast. I saw him picking up all the hunks of green, rotting meat—and *eating* them.

Chapter 3

"SHE'S NOT MY GIRLFRIEND!"

Out in the hall, I turned to my friends Feenman and Crench. "What do you dudes want to do now?" I asked.

Feenman stood there giggling.

"What's so funny?" I asked.

He pointed into the game room. "Your girlfriend is in there."

"Huh? My girlfriend? What are you talking about?"

I peeked inside the room. Jennifer Ecch was smiling at me and throwing big, smoochy kisses.

I groaned. I grabbed my stomach. "Big, smoochy kisses? I'm going to be sick."

How to describe Jennifer Ecch?

She's a foot taller than everyone in school, and twice as wide. She's big and strong. When she walks on the grass, she leaves footprints four inches deep in the ground!

Nightmare Girl.

That's what I call her.

And she's totally in love with me. She calls me Sweet Cakes, and makes loud kissy noises every time she sees me.

How embarrassing is *that*?

Crench tapped my shoulder. "Good luck, Big B. Jennifer Ecch is telling everyone you invited her to the dance."

"Wh~wh~wh~wh."

I couldn't speak. My jaw sank to my knees. I grabbed it and pushed it back up to my chin. "Dance? What dance?" I cried.

"The dance party here at the Student Center," Crench said. "Jennifer Ecch is bragging that you *begged* her to be your date."

"Huh? I'd rather have my nose pierced with a screwdriver!" I cried.

Crench fell on the floor giggling.

"Hee~hee~hee."

Feenman slapped my shoulder. He was giggling, too. "Looks like you're trapped, Big B."

"No way," I said. I turned and saw April-May June in the game room. I guess the hamburger smell cleared up. She was starting a Ping-Pong game with another girl from her dorm.

April-May June. My true love! The hottest, most beautiful, most stuck-up-for-*good*-reason girl at the whole Rotten School.

April-May was my *real* girlfriend. Except she didn't know it yet.

"Don't worry, dudes," I said. "I'll put an end to this Jennifer Ecch thing right away."

Chapter 4

THE MAGIC MOMENT

April-May June zigzagged behind the Ping-Pong table, batting the ball over the net. Her blond ponytail swung behind her. Her friend Sharonda Davis had a wicked serve.

I stepped up to the table and caught the ball in midair. "Time out!" I cried. "You two play like champions! Didn't I see you two playing in the championship on ESPN?"

April-May stuck out her hand. "Bernie, give us back the ball," she said.

"You two are awesome. *Awesome!*" I said, flashing

my dimples at April-May. "I see you've worked up a sweat."

I pulled out a tissue and started mopping April-May's forehead.

She rolled her eyes. "Bernie, give us back the ball."

"Do you play Ping-Pong?" Sharonda asked me.

"Well, yes," I replied. "But my backhand was *outlawed* because no one could return it."

Both girls laughed.

"I'd show you," I said. "But I have to speak privately to April-May." I tugged her away from the table.

She stuck out her hand. "Bernie. The ball."

"I know you want to ask me to the dance party," I said. "But you're too shy, right?"

"Bernie—the ball." She made a grab for it, but I swung it out of her reach.

"It's okay to be shy," I said. "Don't be nervous. The answer is *yes.* I'll go with you."

"Bernie—the ball," she said.

I held the Ping-Pong ball out in front of her. "So the answer is yes? You'll go with me?"

"No way," she replied.

20

"Is that a *maybe?*" I asked.

"Are we going to play or what?" Sharonda called, banging the table with her paddle.

Totally rude.

"No way I'll go with you," April-May said. "You're a troublemaker. I can't go to the dance with a trouble-maker."

I gasped. "Huh? Are you kidding? A trouble-maker? *Me?* I haven't been in trouble since"—I checked my watch—"since four o'clock."

April-May shook her head. "Sorry, Bernie. You don't care about school. All you think about is your-self—and making *money money money* off everyone."

April-May's blue eyes gazed at me coldly, like two frozen lakes. "I need someone I can rely on. Like Sherman Oaks."

Yuccch!

"You *can't* go to a dance party with that rich, spoiled brat!" I cried. "His wallet is so fat, he can't move his leg!"

"Sherman stays out of trouble," April-May said. "And he gets good grades. And he's filthy rich. No offense, but you're just a *loser*, Bernie. You're

gonna be kicked
out of school any day
now. I know Mrs.
Heinie is watching
you carefully."

I staggered back,
grabbing my chest.
"Me? A l-l-loser? I never
heard that word. *Loser?* Did
you just make that word up?"

"Give me the ball, Bernie."
She stuck out her hand.

"Tell you what…," I said.

Tell you what. With those three
words, I changed my whole life.
That's when it started. That was
the magic moment when the new
Bernie was born!

Chapter 5

APRIL-MAY SAYS YES

"Tell you what," I said again. "What if I become the best student in school?"

April-May yawned. "Ha."

"What if I become the best, most straight-arrow student on campus?"

April-May rolled her eyes. "Ha-ha doubled."

"And what if I stay out of trouble for *a whole week*!" I cried.

"Ha-ha *squared*," she replied. "Fat chance, Bernie. What if I flap my arms and fly to Miami?"

Sharonda laughed. She had a *cold* sense of humor.

"It's Tuesday night," I said. "What if I don't break any rules and stay out of trouble till next Monday night?"

Oh, wait. What about the slug race?

No problem. The next slug race wasn't until Tuesday. I could do it. I could be good until next Monday night. It wouldn't be easy, but I could try.

"I'm serious," I told April-May. "What if I stay out of trouble for a whole week—*and* I am a better student than Sherman?"

"Okay. Sure," she said, grinning at Sharonda. "You do that, Bernie. And I'll go to the dance party with you."

"*Awesome!*" I cried.

To celebrate, I tossed the Ping-Pong ball up to the ceiling and then caught it in my teeth. But I was so excited, I swallowed it.

Gulp. I felt it slide down my throat.

Both girls glared at me. "Give us the ball, Bernie."

I shrugged. "Sorry. You'll have to wait a few days for it."

Chapter 6

BELZER HAS A PROBLEM

I started to the door—but stopped when I heard a shout.

"Bernie, my hand is stuck! Help me! I'm *stuck!*"

"Help! Help!"

My pal Belzer!

Why do my friends always call *me* when they're in trouble? Is it because they know I'm a genius?

"Bernie—help me!"

I hurried across the hall. It didn't take long to see the problem.

Belzer was crunched down on his knees. His hand was stuck in the candy bar vending machine. Actually, his *whole arm* was stuck inside the slot.

He turned to me. He had sweat pouring down his chubby face. The poor guy was in pain. "Big B—get me *outta* this!"

I rested my hand on his head. "Belzer, how many

times do I have to tell you? *First,* you put the money in the machine. *Then* you reach for the candy bar. You always do it backwards."

"But, Bernie, you *took* all my money last week—remember?" Belzer whined. "You said you were starting a college fund for me."

"You're nine years old," I said. "You have to start thinking about the future. I put the money in a safe place for you."

"A safe place?"

"Yes. My wallet."

I tugged his shoulder. He let out a cry. The poor guy was really stuck.

"No problem. I'll have you out of there before you can count to a hundred thousand," I said.

He whimpered some more. "Thanks, Big B. But could you do it a little faster? I don't think I can count that high."

"Hmmm…" I stared down at my squirming friend. I put the Bernie Bridges brain into action. And I came up with a plan. A desperate plan. A dangerous plan…

But, I'll do *anything* for my friends!

Chapter 7

My Good Deed

I grabbed my wallet and pulled out a dollar bill. "I'm putting money in the slot," I said. "When I do, the machine will let go of your hand."

I waved the dollar bill in front of his face. "My *own* money," I said. "I'm giving up a *whole dollar* for you, Belzer. That's because I always help out my pals."

"Oh, *thank* you, Bernie," Belzer replied. "Thank you. You're the BEST!"

"And, you don't have to pay back the dollar till you get your allowance," I said.

"Oh, thank you. Thank you!"

I kissed the dollar bill good-bye. Then I slid it into the candy machine.

I heard a few clicks. A squeak. A *thump*.

"Yes!" Belzer cried. He fell over backwards as his arm came sliding out. His hand was wrapped tightly around a Nutty Nutty Bar.

"Wheeeee! I'm free! I'm free!" He kicked his legs in the air and let out a happy cry. Then, still on his back, he ripped the paper wrapper off and jammed the chocolate bar into his mouth.

See? April-May June was wrong about me. I *do* care about other people. I care about my Rotten House buddies. And I don't just think about making money all the time.

I smiled at Belzer, down on the floor, gulping loudly, cramming the chocolate bar down his throat. Yes, Bernie B. had done a good deed tonight. And it gave me a warm feeling, a *good* feeling.

And then I heard a *thud*.

Another Nutty Nutty Bar dropped into the slot. *Thud*. Another one. Then another one.

Thud. Thud. Thud.

A miracle!

"The machine is going wacko!" Belzer cried, his mouth smeared with chocolate.

"Grab them," I said. "Hurry. Grab them all."

See? Do a good deed—and good things happen to *you*! This "being good" idea was *already* starting to pay off!

Thud. Thud. Thudthudthud.

"Grab them! Grab them, Belzer!" I shouted. "We can sell them to the second graders for a dollar each!"

Chapter 8

CRUSHED

My backpack weighed a ton. Belzer had loaded it with Nutty Nutty Bars. I swung it onto my shoulders and headed off to my dorm.

It was a cool, clear night as I strode across the Great Lawn. I passed the statue of the man who had built our school—I.B. Rotten. I squeezed his long nose for good luck.

It was a beautiful night. Crickets chirped. Frogs croaked. The apple trees on the Great Lawn whispered in the breeze.

As I said, I love going to boarding school. I feel

sorry for kids who don't live at school and who have to go home every day.

I could see my dorm, Rotten House, up ahead on the left.

My heart was swelling with joy. I felt total happiness. And all because April-May June had said *yes*, that she'd go to the party with me.

All I had to do was change everything about me. Could I do it?

Could I really stay out of trouble till next Monday night?

Study? Do my homework and be a better student than Sherman Oaks?

A cold sweat broke out on my forehead. My whole body started to tremble.

"You can do it, Bernie," I said, giving myself a pep talk. "After all, it's only a week."

That's what I was thinking when I was hit from behind and crushed by a two-ton army tank.

Chapter 9

SHERMAN SHOWS OFF

"Sorry," a voice said.

I landed flat on my stomach. Spitting out a mouthful of dirt, I slowly raised my head from the grass—and gazed up at Sherman Oaks.

I hadn't been hit by a tank. I'd been run over by the enormous new bike Sherman's parents had sent him. "Unph ungggph," I said.

Sherman grinned down at me with his three hundred teeth. "Sorry," he repeated. "I didn't see you till it was too late. I shouldn't wear these designer, wraparound sunglasses at night. But they're so expensive, I hate to take them off."

"Ungggh Grunnnnph," I said. Everything hurt, but I managed to roll onto my back.

"I put Godzilla in his cage and hurried to get my new bike," Sherman said. "I can't stand to be away from it. It was built by the Hummer company. Would you like to touch it for a few seconds?"

"Grunnnnngh," I replied.

"It has a DVD player, four stereo speakers, and satellite radio," Sherman said. "The handlebars are eighteen-karat gold." He slid his hands up and down them. "Oooh, I love the feel of gold, don't you?"

I spit out some more chunks of dirt.

"And check out the seat," Sherman said. "The seat is made from the fluff of baby chicks. Is that soft, or what? My parents think they can impress me by buying me the best of everything in the world."

With a loud groan, I pulled myself up to a sitting position. The candy bars! I had forgotten about them. Were they crushed?

I swung my backpack to my chest and tugged it open. Thank goodness! The Nutty Nutty Bars were all okay.

"Sherman, would you like to buy some candy bars?" I asked. "I paid two dollars each. But since you're my friend, I'll sell them to you for a dollar fifty. How about it?"

He stared down at me from the fluffy bike seat.

I reached into the backpack. "How many would you like to buy? Ten? Twenty? I'll make you a special deal: Buy twenty and I'll give them to you for only fifty dollars."

Sherman sneered at me. "I don't have time for candy bars," he said. "I have to study for the History test. Everyone expects me to ace it. And I won't let them down. I plan to get the *best* grade in the history of the school."

I snickered. "I'm afraid you'll have to settle for *second* best," I said. "Because *I'm* going to come in first."

Sherman laughed so hard, I think he hurt himself. He grabbed his sides, tears running down his cheeks.

"Thanks for the laugh, Bernie," he said. "You may not be awesomely wealthy like me. But your sense of humor is rich."

"I'm not joking," I said. "I promised April-May June I'd be a better student than you this week. And then she's going with *me* to the dance party."

Sherman raised his dark glasses and squinted at me. "Bernie, do you know how to spell *ha-ha-ha*? I'll give you a hint: It starts with *h-a*."

He sneered again. "*I'm* taking April-May to the party. *No way* you can do better than me this week. I won't let you."

"Okay, it's war," I said.

"Yes. War," he agreed.

"And I'm going to win," I said. "I'm trying a whole new plan. Something I've never tried before."

Sherman grinned at me. "What's that?"

"It's called *studying*," I said.

Sherman tossed back his head and laughed some more. Then he grabbed the handlebars, lowered his shoes to the pedals—and rode over me again as he hurried away.

Chapter 10

CRUSHED, PART TWO

The next morning, Belzer brought me breakfast in bed. He brings it to me every morning, right before he walks my fat bulldog, Gassy.

This morning, Belzer wore his school blazer. And underneath it, a white and gray T-shirt with the words NOSE PICKERS ANONYMOUS across the front.

I didn't ask him about the shirt. I was too busy thinking about my new life as an excellent student. Study, study, study. That was my plan.

I'd even found the school library on a map. I

never knew we *had* a library. I thought it was a storage building!

"*Eat birdseed and choke! Go SWALLOW a cuttle-bone!*"

My adorable parrot, Lippy, was hopping up and down on his perch, trying to get my attention. The cute thing loves to bite my fingers every morning and make them bleed.

"Sorry. No time for you," I called to the parrot.

"Bite my tail feathers!"

Who taught him to say that?

I made my way outside. A warm, sunny day. The Great Lawn sparkling. Birds singing in the trees.

Kids were pouring out of the dorms, heading to the School House, our classroom building. We also like to call it the Mouse House. Guess why: All the mice in town go there for their winter vacation. Summer vacation, too. (And spring and fall.)

I started to trot. I wanted to be early to class. I wanted to cling to every word Mrs. Heinie said.

But I didn't make it. I was halfway across the campus when I was hit from behind and crushed by a two-ton army tank.

Chapter 11

JENNIFER ATTACKS

No. This time it wasn't Sherman Oaks on his bike. With a painful groan, I turned and saw Jennifer Ecch hulking over me.

She rolled me onto my back and sat down on my stomach.

"Good morning to you, too," I gasped.

Have you ever seen an elephant sitting on a mouse? It isn't a pretty picture.

"I want to talk to you," she said. Her bangs covered her eyes. She looked like a sheepdog in a dress. I hoped she didn't have fleas!

"I can't really talk right now," I whispered. "Because you're cutting off all my breath."

She shifted her weight. I felt a couple of ribs crack.

"Honey Buns, I've been telling *everyone* you're taking me to the dance party," she said. "So...*will* you?"

"*Please* don't call me Honey Buns," I begged.

She pressed all her weight down on me. "Will you take me to the party?"

"I wish I could," I said, trying to sound sincere. "I really do. But April-May already asked me."

"Huh?" Jennifer let out a startled cry and jumped to her feet. She pulled me up and twisted my arm behind my back. "I don't believe you," she said.

She pulled my arm up until I heard a loud *snap*. "I swear. It's true," I groaned.

"There's no *way* April-May will go with you," Jennifer said, giving my arm another hard tug. "I'll be waiting and watching, Bernie. And I'll be ready for you at the Student Center when April-May goes to the party with someone else."

"Ohhh, my arm. My arm," I wailed.

Her mouth dropped open. "Oh. Did I hurt you, Sweet Cakes? Let me make it better." She started kissing my arm up and down.

Lots of kids stopped to watch.

It's SO EMBARRASSING to have a girl in love with you in fourth grade!

I broke away and went running to class, cradling my arm in my other hand.

Now I knew I *had* to be a better student than Sherman. I had to show April-May that I was the class genius.

It was the only way to stay out of Jennifer Ecch's clutches. The only way to keep her from breaking the rest of my bones!

Chapter 12

My First Night as a Bookworm

Wednesday night, I was sitting at a table in the library, leaning over my History textbook. Studying, studying. I'd been sitting there for nearly an hour—a new world's record for Bernie B.

I glanced up to rest my eyes—and saw Feenman and Crench running up to me. They looked confused. I knew they'd never been here before.

"Look at all the books!" Feenman said. "Is this like a bookstore or something?"

"Bernie, where were you this afternoon?" Crench asked. "We were supposed to have our afternoon study group—studying SpongeBob cartoons on TV."

"Sorry," I said. "I was here in the library, reading chapters for the History test."

Feenman squinted at me. "Yeah, sure, Bernie. What kind of scheme are you cooking up? Something to make Sherman look like a jerk?"

"No. I'm serious," I said. "I'm studying."

"Are you sick or something?" Crench asked. He put his hand on my forehead.

"I'm not sick," I said, shoving his sweaty hand away. "I have to study hard. I have to be good, dudes. I promised April-May I'd be good all week."

"Bernie, this is no time to be good," Feenman said. "Sherman is holding a pool tournament, and he's *killing* everyone."

"He's using that new digital pool cue his parents sent him," Crench said. "It has some kind of radar on it. It can't miss! Hurry—you've gotta come win for us, Big B!"

Tempting. Very tempting. I started to get up.

But then I saw April-May sitting at a nearby table. And I shouted—just loud enough for her to hear—"*Are you guys kidding me? Play POOL when I could be studying the history of Panama? Go away!"*

Feenman and Crench stared at me. "We're worried about you, Bernie," Crench said. "You never tried to be good before. It's not like you!"

"I did a good deed last night," I said, "and it paid off big-time—with tons of candy bars. Get used to the *new* Bernie, dudes."

I made sure April-May was listening. Then I shouted, "Listen, *dudes, I'm in school to LEARN. I wish I had time to stay in the library and read ALL these books!"*

I smiled at April-May—*and she smiled back!*
She was *buying* it!

Feenman and Crench slumped out, muttering and shaking their heads.

I buried my head in the textbook and started to read again. I moved my lips so April-May could see that I was concentrating hard.

It's starting to work, I thought. *She's starting to see what an awesome student I am. Now I need to do a few more good deeds to impress her....*

Chapter 13

HOW I IMPRESSED APRIL-MAY

On Thursday night, I crept out of Rotten House around nine o'clock. I made sure no one was watching. I carried a big bag of trash out of the dorm.

Time to do another good deed.

I carried the trash onto the Great Lawn and scattered it all around.

I knew April-May would be passing this way soon. She always took this path from the library to the girls' dorm.

"April-May, get ready to be impressed," I murmured softly, tossing the garbage under the bushes.

"Get ready to see what an awesome, good guy Bernie B. is!"

A few minutes later, I saw her coming toward me on the path.

"Showtime!" I whispered.

I bent down and started gathering up the trash.

Humming to myself, I stuffed pieces of trash back into the plastic trash bag.

"Bernie!" April-May cried. "What are you doing out here so late?"

I stuffed a few more pieces of garbage into the bag. Then I raised my head and flashed her a smile.

"I hate litter," I said. "Our school is so beautiful. I want to keep it looking perfect. So I come out here every night and pick up the trash."

April-May gazed hard at me. She didn't say a word. But I knew she was totally impressed.

She could see what a good person I am.

She trotted away. I waited until she was out of sight.

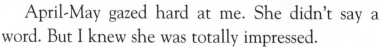

Then I called to Belzer, who was hiding behind a tree, "Okay—you can pick the trash up now. I'm going to sleep!"

I wasn't finished impressing April-May. The next morning, I got my Rotten House buddy Nosebleed to help me do another good deed.

Nosebleed is a skinny little guy with one major talent. You can probably figure it out from his name. That's right. Just look at him funny—and he gets a nosebleed!

I brought Nosebleed to the front of the girls' dorm. The dorm has no name. No one ever thought of a name for it. It's just called the girls' dorm.

Anyway, I brought Nosebleed there and waited until I saw April-May come out the front door. Then I picked him up and started to run with him in my arms.

April-May ran after me. "Bernie—what are you doing?" she called.

"I'm rushing Nosebleed to the nurse," I said. "He has a bad nosebleed."

I turned back to her and shrugged. "I'll be late to

class," I said. "But I gotta take care of my friends. My friends are the most important thing to me. It's just the way I am."

April-May grabbed my arm. "But, Bernie—his nose isn't bleeding."

I frowned at Nosebleed. "Hey, what's *wrong* with you? Start bleeding! Bleed for her!"

I turned to April-May. "See what I have to put up with?"

Chapter 14

I'M TENSE

One hour before the History test. The pressure was on. I admit it. Even Bernie Bridges felt a little tense.

The Rotten House dorm has a Study Hall Room downstairs. I went there to study because I knew it would be quiet. No one has used this room in a hundred years.

I pushed away the cobwebs. Then I hunched over the table. My eyes scanned the History textbook. I knew the imports and exports of every country in South America.

But my brain was *fried* from all this studying.

Does tin come from Bolivia or Peru? Are the jute mines in Chile or Paraguay? And what the heck is *jute*?

How could I keep it all straight?

I looked up and saw Mrs. Heinie staring at me. Her eyes bulged behind her thick glasses. Her mouth was open in surprise.

"Bernie? You're in the Study Hall Room?" she said. "Should I call for the nurse?"

"I'm studying for the History test," I said. "It's important to be an outstanding student."

"I'd better call the nurse," Mrs. H. said. "You must have a high fever. You're talking crazy."

"No, I'm not," I said. I jumped to my feet and shook her hand. "You've inspired me, Mrs. Heinie. You've set the right example for me. Thanks to you, I want to spend my life learning, learning, LEARNING."

"Now I *know* you're sick," Mrs. Heinie replied. "Now I'm *really* going to keep an eye on you, Bernie."

Chapter 15

I'M HOT!

I felt too tense. I was nervous about the History test. And the strain of being good all week was starting to give me the shakes.

I had to get loose. I walked over to the Fitness Center. Belzer carried my History textbook for me.

Sherman Oaks's parents had built the Fitness Center. It has all the latest equipment. I heard that Sherman Oaks works out for an hour before every test. He says it gets the juices flowing.

That's what I wanted to do. Flowing juices had to be good for test-taking. A little work on the treadmill.

Get the heart pumping on the stationary bike. Maybe lift some weights…

So where was Sherman? I didn't see him anywhere. Instead, I saw two girls come rushing in—Flora and Fauna, the Peevish twins.

These two sisters are almost as stuck-up as Sherman. I guess that's why they always hang out with him.

"Bernie, we were looking for you," Fauna said.

"Where is your friend Sherman?" I asked. "Hiding in his room because he knows *I'm* going to score higher on the History test?"

They both sneered at me as if I were a fly that should be swatted. "Sherman is way too rich to even *think* about you," Fauna said.

"He's doing that secret thing that he does," Flora said. "Ever since he started doing it, he gets a perfect score on every test."

"Huh?" I let out a gasp. *Secret thing?* I grabbed Flora's arm. "What is it?"

Both girls shook their heads. "We can't tell you. It's a secret thing."

I turned to Belzer. "Reach into my backpack," I said. "Pull out what's in there."

I turned to the Peevish twins. "How about a dozen Nutty Nutty Bars? Would you tell me Sherman's secret for a dozen Nutty Nutty Bars?"

They looked at each other. "A dozen *each?*" Flora asked.

"Okay, okay." I tossed them each a dozen Nutty Nutty Bars.

"Here's the secret," Fauna said. "Sherman wraps a hot hot hot towel around his head. He keeps it burning hot."

"It does something to his brain cells," Flora said. "It gets his brain cells moving faster. And he never misses a question."

The Peevish sisters hurried away with their candy bars.

I turned to Belzer. "Don't just stand there. Hurry! Hot towels! I need burning hot towels!"

"But—but—where?" Belzer cried.

"The laundry," I said. "Get to the laundry. Hurry. I need those hot towels. Gotta get those brain cells moving!"

A few minutes later, Belzer came running back into the gym. He had an armload of towels, and he was screaming in pain. "Ow! Ow! They're hot! They're burning hot!"

He had burns over most of his body. "Good work, Belzer," I said. "Quick. Wrap one around my head."

As soon as the scalding hot towel touched my skin, I could feel my brain come alive. "Yes! Yes! This is awesome, Belzer. More towels! Get more towels! I'm going to ace this test!"

My head throbbed. I wanted to scream in pain. But I let the heat soak into my brain.

My head was red and swollen when I walked into the classroom.

But I knew I had the History test aced. I could already see my perfect score.

I took my seat and heard someone call my name. I turned to see Sherman run into the room, followed by Miss Hanley, the school nurse. "There he is!" Sherman cried. "Check him out."

Nurse Hanley strode over, her eyes studying me. "Sherman says you're very sick and shouldn't be in class today."

I jumped to my feet. "Huh? Me, sick? That's crazy!"

"He's totally sick," Sherman said. "Look at his head. It's all red and swollen."

Nurse Hanley felt my forehead. "OH, MY!" she screamed. "You're *burning up*! I've never *felt* a head this hot! You must have a fever of 106!"

"But—but—but—" I sputtered. "I wrapped hot towels around my head."

"You're talking crazy," Nurse Hanley said. "It must be the fever. Let's get you to a bed in the infirmary!" She dragged me out of the room.

I turned and saw the big grin on Sherman's face. "Bye, Bernie. Feel better soon!" he called. "Guess you won't be scoring higher than me after all!"

Chapter 16

THE DOUBLE-
SMART QUIZ BOWL

The next morning, Nurse Hanley let me go back to the dorm. Feenman and Crench came running into my room. "Are you okay, Bernie?" Feenman asked. "Did the fever break?"

"There *was* no fever," I grumbled. "Sherman pulled that hot-towel trick on me. He made sure I couldn't beat him on the test. He doesn't want me to take April-May to the party."

"We ate your breakfast," Crench said. "We didn't think you were coming back."

"Thanks for trying to cheer me up," I said.

"We ate some Nutty Nutty Bars, too," Feenman said. "Just nine or ten."

I barely heard him. I was miserable. *Miserable!* Because of Sherman's dirty trick, I had missed the History test. How would I ever impress April-May now?

I stepped over to the window and peered down to the yard. I could see Jennifer Ecch down there. She had set up a tent outside Rotten House so she could spy on me twenty-four hours a day.

There she was, staring up from the tent flaps. Just watching…and waiting.

Waiting to carry me to the dance party like a big hunting dog with a rabbit in her teeth.

Gulp. I had to think of a new plan to impress April-May—FAST!

I changed into my school uniform. Then I sneaked out the back door so Jennifer wouldn't see me.

I was halfway across the Great Lawn, thinking

hard…thinking…when I was run over from behind by a two-ton tank.

I heard Sherman's giggle. I looked up from the grass and saw Sherman and Flora Peevish. He was giving her a lift on the back of his huge, eighteen-karat-gold bike.

Sherman leaned over the handlebars and grinned down at me. "Hope you're feeling better, Bernie! We missed you in History class!" He and Flora burst out laughing.

I ignored their laughter. No way could I stoop to their level.

I reached for my backpack. "How many Nutty Nutty Bars do you want today?" I asked Sherman. "I'll give you a special price since you're such a good friend. Only three dollars a bar."

"Sherman and I don't have time for candy," Flora sneered. "We've entered the Double-Smart Quiz Bowl together."

"It's two kids on a team," Sherman said. "It's only for smart kids. You can watch from the audience, Bernie. I'm sure someone will sound out the big words for you."

They both laughed again. They slapped each other high fives and nearly fell off the bike.

But I was thinking hard....

April-May would be *totally* impressed if I won the Double-Smart Quiz Bowl. *Much* better than beating Sherman in a stupid History test!

"You two should give up now," I told Flora and Sherman. "It's all over. You don't stand a chance—because I'm entering the contest!"

They both tossed back their heads and laughed some more. They laughed until a fly flew into Flora's mouth and she started to gag. She coughed it out as

Sherman rode over me on the bike and pedaled away.

I had thick black tire marks across my school blazer. But I didn't care. I had a plan. I knew how to win.

Chapter 17

BILLY THE BRAIN

After school, I grabbed Billy the Brain and dragged him to the library. Billy has a solid C-minus average. That's why everyone at Rotten School calls him the Brain.

He's a totally awesome student. Some nights he studies for almost half an hour. And he reads books that don't have pictures in them.

So I knew he'd be the *perfect* partner for the Double-Smart Quiz Bowl.

"We can't lose," I told him. We huddled in a corner of the library. "I brought some sample questions.

I know they'll be easy for you."

He shrugged. "Whatever."

"Okay. Try these," I said. I raised the sheets of paper I'd brought. "Who was the fortieth president of the United States?"

Billy rubbed his chin. "Walt Disney?"

"That was too easy," I said. "Let's go to the next one. What does H_2O stand for?"

Billy rubbed his chin again. "Salt?"

"We'll come back to that one," I said. I scanned the page of questions. "Here's one you'll know. What is the capital of Illinois?"

Billy shut his eyes and thought hard. "Is it South Dakota?"

I shoved the questions into my backpack. "That's enough for tonight," I said.

Billy rubbed his temples. "That gave me such a headache," he said.

Uh-oh. Have I made a mistake? I wondered. Should we change his nickname to "Billy the Total Moron"?

I hoped not. I needed Billy. I needed him to be brilliant, to help me win the contest and impress April-May.

Billy hurried away, rubbing his aching head.

I started to get up, but I stopped when I saw two eyes staring at me from behind a bookshelf.

Jennifer Ecch poked her enormous head through the shelf, knocking about a dozen books to the floor. "I'm watching you, Bernie," she said. "I'm watching and I'm waiting. And I'm ready for the dance party."

She reached through the shelf, grabbed my hand, and licked my face.

I've got to win that contest tomorrow, I told myself.

If I don't, there will be a lot more licking at the party.

I finally tugged free of Jennifer's grasp. My face was sopping wet.

"See you at the party, Honey Cakes," she whispered.

No way. I planned to study all night. By tomorrow, I'd be *brilliant!*

Unfortunately, my plan didn't work out. That night, I made a horrible mistake.

Chapter 18

A CHAMPION SLUG

That night in the dorm, I couldn't find anyone to help quiz me. Belzer, Feenman, and Crench weren't in their room.

I asked Nosebleed to help me. But he got a nosebleed and had to run to the nurse.

My friend Chipmunk said he'd help. Chipmunk is the shyest, quietest guy in school. He started reading me questions. But he muttered them into his hand, and I couldn't hear a word he said.

Finally, I had to toss him out of my room. "Thanks for your help, dude," I told him. "But a little advice… You're supposed to *exhale* when you talk—not *inhale!*"

"I'll practice," he said. At least, that's what I *think* he said.

I decided to quiz myself. But Lippy, my adorable parrot, started making a racket. "*Go swallow a cuttlebone! Eat birdseed and DIE!*"

Cute guy. But I had no time for him tonight. I pulled the cover over his cage. "*Come closer and I'll BITE your throat!*" he squawked.

He's so playful.

I sat down at my desk and started looking at some quiz books I'd found in the library. But before I could really get down to work, Feenman and Crench came bursting into the room.

"Bernie—hurry!" Feenman cried, pulling me to my feet. "You've gotta get to the Student Center!"

"Sherman is having a slug

race!" Crench said. "He's cheating. He's not waiting till Tuesday. You gotta get Sluggo there or Sherman will win."

I sat back down. "Not tonight, fellas," I said. "You know I promised to be good for a week. I have to stay here and study."

Their mouths dropped open. "Study?" Crench cried. "Didn't you hear me? The race is starting in a few minutes!"

I shook my head. "Not for Bernie B. I'm studying for the Quiz Bowl tomorrow. Dudes, I have to win that contest. I have to beat Sherman and impress April-May."

Feenman grabbed my shoulders. "You don't understand, Big B. Sherman has a brand-new racing slug. He is bragging to everyone. He says it can beat Sluggo by a mile!"

"Huh?" I jumped angrily to my feet. "Sherman is insulting Sluggo? The greatest racing slug in the history of Rotten School sports? He *dares* to insult the Great Sluggo?"

They both nodded.

I slammed my book shut. I started for the door. "Crench—get Sluggo from his cage!" I cried. "Let's go, guys. Gentle. Be gentle! That slug is a champion!"

Chapter 19

THE GOOD, THE BAD AND THE VERY SLIMY

When I trotted into the game room, the guys were all there. All the same guys from Tuesday night. They were putting the slugs through their warm-up exercises.

Sherman couldn't wait to show off his new slug. "Check him out. He's a Chinese razor slug. My father brought him home from Hong Kong. He cost two thousand dollars."

Two thousand dollars for a slug?

I studied it. It looked like it had tiny, pointed teeth in its head. Impossible. A slug with teeth?

"Sherman," I said, "it looks like *you* when you wake up in the morning—except it's not as slimy!"

Everyone laughed but Sherman.

"Let's see who's laughing at the end of the race," Sherman said.

Again, we each bet five dollars. I closed the game room door so we wouldn't be bothered by any intruders. We moved to the end of the table to line up our slugs.

I massaged Sluggo's back and gave him a pep talk. "You're a champ! You're the MVP!" I said.

He squirted out something gooey in my hand.

"Oh, wow!" Beast let out a groan. "Oh, wow. Oh, wow. I *stepped* on mine!"

Beast pulled up his big foot. "Aw, look," he groaned. "It's stuck to the bottom of my boot." He pried the dead slug off the boot, held it up—and popped it into his mouth.

I grabbed my stomach. "Is that gross enough for everyone?" I asked.

Beast was still chewing. "Kinda salty," he said.

"My razor slug is getting impatient," Sherman said. "Let's start the race."

We lined up the slugs. I started to count down. "Ready…set…"

Sluggo started early. I had to pull him back. He is a champ, but he always wants to cheat.

"Ready…set…WAIT!" I cried. "This is *wrong!*"

I lifted Sluggo from the table. They were all staring at me.

I suddenly remembered April-May and my promise to her. I had no choice. I promised I'd be good for a week. To stay out of trouble. To be better than Sherman.

And Bernie B. never breaks a promise.

I'd almost slipped. I'd almost made a terrible mistake. But I caught myself in time.

"No race tonight. I've gotta go, guys," I said. I started to the door.

"Bernie—are you *crazy?*" Sherman cried. "You can't walk out."

"I have to," I said. "My studies are much more important. I'm here to learn. I'm here to educate myself. I'm going to beat you tomorrow at the Double-Smart Quiz Bowl."

"Huh? He's SICK!" Joe Sweety muttered.

I opened my mouth to answer—but stopped when I heard a loud knock on the door.

Silence fell over the room.

"What's going on in there?" a voice called.

Mrs. Heinie! Again!

"We're busted," Wes Updood said.

We all froze.

The game room door swung open. Mrs. Heinie burst in. She gazed around the room. "Why was that door closed?" she demanded. "What are you boys *doing* in here again?"

Chapter 20

BERNIE THINKS FAST

I'm doomed, I thought.

Doomed.

Mrs. Heinie will drag me to Headmaster Upchuck's office. April-May will go to the dance with Sherman. I'll be stuck with Jennifer Ecch—forever!

What can I do? Can I talk my way out of this?

In a total panic, I swept up all the slugs. I hid them carefully in my fists. Then I hid my fists behind my back. I turned and saw Mrs. Heinie staring at me.

"I know *you're* behind this, Bernie," she said.

"What are you up to?"

I flashed her my innocent smile, the one with the dimples twinkling in both cheeks. "We're planning something for your birthday, Mrs. H.," I said. "You're special to us, and we want to get you a really good present."

She squinted through her thick glasses. "What are those wet, slimy tracks on the table?" she asked.

"Those are my tears," I said. "I get so *emotional* when I think about your birthday."

Mrs. Heinie stared at me. "Really? You boys are talking about my birthday?"

"We want to get you something shiny," I said. "Because you make our lives shine every day."

Yuck. Was I spreading it a little *too* thick?

No. She was buying it.

A warm smile spread over Mrs. Heinie's face. "That's so sweet," she said. "Thank you, boys. I'll see you Rotten House guys back at the dorm."

She turned and started to leave.

Bernie B. does it again!

I was so happy, I jumped up and pumped my fists in the air to celebrate my victory.

Mrs. Heinie turned around. "Bernie? What do you have in your hands?" she asked.

Uh-oh. I celebrated too soon.

"Um…nothing," I said. "I just like to make fists every night. It's an exercise I learned from Coach Bunz."

She squinted through her glasses at my closed fists. "Open up," she said. "Let's take a look."

"Nothing in them," I said. "Coach Bunz says if you make a fist for an hour, it strengthens the knuckles. And that's what I want—really strong knuckles."

"Open your hands," Mrs. H. demanded. "You're hiding something."

I had no choice. Slowly, I opened both fists.

Mrs. H. grabbed hold of my hands. "Oh, my!" she cried. "Your hands are cold and damp and slimy. Bernie—you're *sick*!"

"No way," I said. "Me? Sick?"

"Your hands are squishy and wet and disgusting! I've never felt *sick hands* like those in my life!" Mrs. Heinie cried. "Come on. I'm taking you to the nurse—right now. March!"

I know when I'm defeated. I didn't fight her. As she dragged me to the door, I slipped the slugs to Beast.

"Bye, Bernie," Sherman called. "Sorry you'll be missing the Double-Smart Quiz Bowl tomorrow!"

I didn't turn back. I didn't want to see the grin on Sherman's face.

Okay, Sherman, I thought. *You asked for it. No more Mr. Nice Guy. This war isn't over. It has just begun....*

Chapter 21

THE OLD GARDEN HOSE TRICK

When Nurse Hanley finally let me out of the infirmary the next afternoon, Feenman and Crench were there to greet me.

Feenman handed me a Nutty Nutty Bar.

"No thanks," I muttered.

"How are you feeling, Big B?" Crench asked.

"How do you *think* I feel?" I snapped. "I missed the Quiz Bowl this morning."

Feenman shook his shaggy head. "At least Sherman doesn't have his fancy Chinese razor slug anymore."

"Why? What happened?" I asked.

"Beast ate him," Feenman said. "Beast liked the first slug so much, he ate all the rest. Sluggo, too."

I sighed. "Too bad. Sluggo was a real thoroughbred. But I've got other problems. See you later, dudes."

I walked on across the Great Lawn. A few minutes later, April-May appeared. Her blond hair blew like a halo behind her. Her blue eyes stared coldly at me. "I guess you messed up, Bernie," she said. "Totally."

I gulped. "You mean because I missed the History test and the Quiz Bowl?"

She nodded. "You promised to be a better student than Sherman. But you didn't keep your promise. That's why I'm going to the dance party with him."

I gulped again. I tried to think of something smart to say. But for the first time in my life, nothing came to me.

"April-May, I have one more day," I said finally. "One last day to prove I'm a better student than Sherman. I'll do it. No problem. Really. You'll see."

"Ha-ha and ha some more," April-May said. She

stuck her tongue out, made a loud spitting noise, and hurried away.

I saw Jennifer Ecch hiding behind a bush. Listening. Watching. Waiting to grab me.

I'm doomed, I thought. *All because of Sherman.*

Sherman had played *two* dirty tricks on me. How did he have the *nerve?*

Who is the KING of dirty tricks around here? Bernie Bridges, of course!

Being a goody-goody wasn't working out for me. I knew I had to go back to being myself.

If only there was a way to get Sherman into *major* trouble. Then April-May would have no choice. She'd have to go to the dance party with me.

But what could I do to get Sherman in trouble?

I was thinking so hard, I didn't see the garden hose on the grass. I tripped over it and fell to my knees.

"Be careful," one of the gardeners called. He was rolling up the fat garden hose. The apple trees all glistened from being watered. The blue-uniformed gardeners were hurrying off to lunch.

"Stay away from that hose," the gardener called

to me. "It's very powerful. It could blast you into the trees." He hurried to catch up to the others.

Did he say, "blast you into the trees"?

Suddenly, I had an idea. Okay, Sherman, old pal—let's see who plays the best dirty tricks on this campus!

"Sherman! Hey—Sherman!" I shouted. I saw him across the grass, showing off his new bike to a group of third-grade girls.

"Sherman—come over here! I have a surprise for you!"

Chapter 22

VICTORY!

Sherman parked the bike against a tree. "What's up, Bernie? Want to touch my bike? If you wash your hands, I'll let you touch it."

I handed him the nozzle of the garden hose. "Headmaster Upchuck wants you to test this hose," I said. "I *begged* him to let *me* do it. But he has this silly idea that *you* are more responsible."

"Of course I am," Sherman replied. He gripped the silvery nozzle. "What does Headmaster Upchuck want me to do?"

"He wants you to test the power," I said. "In a few

minutes, he's going to send a guy over." I bent down and picked up one of the gardeners' caps. "The dude will be wearing a red cap just like this one. When you see him coming, let him have it with the hose—full blast."

Sherman squinted at me. "That doesn't make any sense, Bernie. Why does the Headmaster want me to blast the guy?"

I shrugged. "Do I know? I'm just passing along his message. Upchuck said it's an important hose test." I grabbed for the nozzle. "Want *me* to do it, Sherman?"

"No way," Sherman said, pulling the hose away from me. "I'm the responsible one. I'll blast the guy."

"Okay. Wait here," I said.

Part One of my plan was working. Now for Part Two.

I hurried off to find Headmaster Upchuck. I knew he had lunch at the Dining Hall every day at this time. Sure enough, I found him climbing the Dining Hall steps.

Headmaster Upchuck is a tiny, little man. The teachers are always mistaking him for one of the students. He's bald and stooped. He's so short, he doesn't even have a shadow!

"I need to see you, sir," I said.

His whole body started to shake. He always starts to shake when he sees me. "What is it *this* time, Bernie?" he asked.

"An emergency, sir," I replied. "The gardeners need you. They have a problem with the apple trees."

He raised his hands to his cheeks. "Not the apple trees!" he cried. "Those are my favorites."

"You'd better go see them, sir. Right away," I said. "And here, put on this red cap. It will protect you from falling apples."

"Thank you, Bernie." He pulled the cap on his head and went running across the grass toward the apple trees.

Of course, I followed close behind. I wouldn't miss this for the world!

Headmaster Upchuck ran across the Great Lawn as fast as his little legs would carry him. As soon as he reached the path through the trees, Sherman raised the hose and let him have it—full blast.

Headmaster Upchuck let out an "Urk! Urk!" sound as the spray hit him in the chest. It knocked him over and sent him sliding on his back across the grass.

"Urk! Urk!"

Sherman kept the hose on him. The Headmaster sputtered and sputtered. Wave after wave of water splashed over him. He thrashed his arms and legs, struggling to stand up, choking and coughing.

"Urk! Urk!"

Finally, some kids rescued him and pulled him to his feet. He was soaked. The back of his suit oozed wet mud.

"Uh-oh," I heard Sherman say. His last words.

Sherman dropped the hose.

A few seconds later, the Headmaster grabbed Sherman by his collar and dragged him off to his office.

Sherman was dead meat.

April-May and I watched Headmaster Upchuck pull Sherman away. I turned to her. "I don't know what got into that guy," I said. "I guess he isn't as good as we thought. I guess he's a big troublemaker."

"Weird," April-May said, shaking her head.

I flashed her my warmest, most sincere grin. "He'll probably be tossed out of school," I said. "So now you'll go with *me* to the dance party?"

She thought about it for a long time. Then she sighed. "Yes," she said. "A deal is a deal. Yes. I'll go with you."

She said YES!

Victory!

Victory for Bernie B.!

Dazed, my heart pounding, I saw Feenman and Crench running up to me. "Bernie, you'd better hurry. Mrs. Heinie wants to see you at the dorm."

Crench shook his head. "I think you're in trouble, Bernie," he said.

"Huh? Me? In trouble? I've been perfect all week," I said.

I turned to April-May. "Wait here. I'll be right back."

But I was wrong. Very wrong.

Chapter 23

MRS. HEINIE STEPS IN

Mrs. Heinie was waiting for me in the front hall at Rotten House. She put a hand on my shoulder and led me into the Study Hall.

"You're looking wonderful today, Mrs. H.," I said. "I love those earrings. The way they droop down to your shoulders. Are they new?"

"I'm not wearing earrings," she said.

Uh-oh. I'd never realized she was a little long in the earlobe department.

"I suppose you want me to tell you about your birthday present," I said. "I know, I know. You don't want us boys to spend too much money on you. But we *want* to. We—"

Mrs. Heinie clamped a hand over my mouth. "Bernie, I want to know what you are up to," she said.

"Mmmmmpph mmph,"

I replied. She still had her hand over my mouth.

"Come clean, Bernie," she said. "What are you planning to pull on us? I know it's something *big*."

"Pull? Planning? Me?" I cried. "I've been an *angel* for days."

"That's what I mean," she said. "I've been watching you, Bernie. A bunch of guys had a pool tournament after Lights-Out—and you weren't there. Some guys were caught playing cards this week— and you weren't there."

"I know—" I started. "You see—"

"Bernie, I saw you reading *books* in the *library*. Don't deny it. I even caught you *studying* in this Study Hall. You've been acting like a perfect student. So I know something is up. I know you're

planning something *big*."

She grabbed me by my school blazer collar. "What is it, Bernie? Confess!"

"I'm just trying to get a good education, Mrs. Heinie," I said. "I want to make you proud of me."

"That PROVES it!" she cried, squeezing my lapels. "You ARE planning something evil!"

"But—but—" I sputtered.

"I won't let you get away with it, Bernie," Mrs. Heinie cried. "You're grounded. You're grounded here in the dorm for a week!"

"But—but—"

"You heard me," she said. "I'm spoiling your evil plans. You're grounded for a week. And one more thing…"

"What's *that?*" I asked weakly.

"Don't ever let me catch you in the library again!"

Chapter 24

COULD IT GET
ANY WORSE?

So, I missed the dance party.

The next morning, I was lying in bed, moaning, staring at the ceiling, thinking dark thoughts.

Feenman and Crench came into my room. "How's it going, Big B?" Feenman asked.

"Shut up," I said.

"That bad, huh."

"Just give me the bad news," I groaned. "Who did April-May go to the party with?"

"She went with Sherman," Crench said.

"Huh? Sherman?" I gasped.

Crench nodded. "April-May said she changed her mind about who she likes. Now she only likes guys who are reckless and live on the edge. Guys who don't care about school, and who get in trouble."

"YAAAAIIIII."

I let out a scream. Then I started punching my pillow. I punched the pillow till Feenman and Crench took the hint and left.

Could it get any worse?

Yes.

I was still punching the pillow when Jennifer Ecch arrived.

She took the pillow away from me. "Don't feel bad, Bernie," she said sweetly. "We only missed one dance. We'll have next week and the next week... and the next week...and the next week...and the next.... Just the two of us!"

HERE'S A SNEAK PEEK AT BOOK #4 IN

R.L. STINE'S

ROTTEN SCHOOL

HONEY BUCKET HAS AN IDEA

My shoes pounded the grass as I took off, running full speed across the school grounds.

I could hear Jennifer Ecch's thundering footsteps close behind me. She was catching up fast. No way could I outrun her.

I call her Nightmare Girl. But that's just being nice.

Jennifer is big and strong. Someone told me she lifts weights *in her sleep*! Yes, she's big and strong and strange. And she's totally in love with me.

How embarrassing is that?

I could see my dorm up ahead. Safety!

But Jennifer was too fast for me. I felt her hot breath on the back of my neck. Then I felt her powerful arms wrap around my waist.

I let out a helpless cry as she tackled me from behind.

I went down hard. I landed on my face. Then the rest of me hit the grass.

I didn't see stars. I didn't see anything. I wondered if I had grass stains on my teeth.

I felt a crushing weight on top of me.

When I opened my eyes, I was sprawled flat on my back and Jennifer was sitting on my chest. "Hi, Bernie," she said. "How's it going?"

"Everything's great," I gasped. "I'm sure I'll start breathing again in a day or so."

She had knitting needles in her hands and a ball of puke-green wool. "What are you doing?" I choked out. I heard some of my ribs cracking under her weight.

"I'm knitting you a sweater, Sweet Cakes," Jennifer said.

"Please, *please* don't call me Sweet Cakes," I begged.

"Okay, Honey Bucket."

I didn't hear that. Oh, please—tell me I didn't hear her call me that!

"I'm knitting a sweater for you in Ms. Monella's Homemaker class," Jennifer said. She poked me in the side with one of the knitting needles. "I need your help. I need to bring you to class and measure you."

Yikes. Can you think of anything more embarrassing than that?

I must have blacked out for a moment. Jennifer kept talking and poking me with the needle. But her voice faded out. I couldn't hear her.

Suddenly, I woke up. And an awesome idea popped into my head. "Jennifer—do it again!" I cried.

She stared down at me with her one blue eye and one brown eye. "Do what, Sweetie Lamb?"

"Tackle me," I said. "Tackle me again!"

She climbed up and pulled me to my feet. I started to breathe again. It felt good. Breathing is good.

"You want me to tackle you again?" Jennifer asked, scratching her brown bangs with a knitting needle.

I nodded, turned, and took off. I ducked my head into the wind and ran full speed over the grass.

ABOUT THE AUTHOR

R.L. Stine graduated from the Rotten School with a solid D+ average, which put him at the top of his class. He says that his favorite activities at school were Scratching Body Parts and Making Armpit Noises.

In sixth grade, R.L. won the school Athletic Award for his performance in the Wedgie Championships. Unfortunately, after the tournament, his underpants had to be surgically removed.

After graduation, R.L. became well known for writing scary book series such as The Nightmare Room, Fear Street, Goosebumps, and Mostly Ghostly, and a short story collection called *Beware!*

Today, R.L. lives in New York City, where he is busy writing stories about his school days.

For more information about R.L. Stine,
go to www.rottenschool.com
and www.rlstine.com

And once again, I heard Jenn. hoofbeats close in on me. She tackle. behind, and I hit the grass with a loud

This time I *did* see stars.

Moaning, I climbed to my feet. "Do it said. "Tackle me again."

This time, I didn't run in a straight line. I and zagged, cutting from one side to the other. Jennifer brought me down in a hard tackle th buried me six inches in the dirt.

Now *everything* hurt. Every part of my body. Even my *shirt* hurt, and it isn't part of me!

I turned to Jennifer. "I'm a genius! You are going to turn the Apples into *Killers*!"

Jennifer closed her blue eye and squinted at me with the brown eye. "But, Honey Bucket—what about my sweater?"

I grinned at her. "Jennifer, when the Apples win the state championship, I'll let you knit me TEN sweaters!"